VICTORIA
FLIES HIGH

VICTORIA FLIES HIGH

Becky Ayres
PICTURES BY
Robin Michal Koontz

COBBLEHILL BOOKS
Dutton · New York

"Hey, Victoria Beasley!" shouted Arnold Kropper. "You don't expect to win the kite-flying contest with that thing, do you?"

"It might not win the contest, but it can beat yours any day," Victoria answered as she hurried into the fairgrounds.

She moved carefully past the cake judging and the popcorn wagon. She was just passing the magic show when a foot shot out of the crowd, and the next moment Victoria was lying on top of her kite.

"Lizards and lemondrops! That was the meanest trick I ever saw," said a voice behind her. "May I be of assistance? The Great Orsini, Magician Extraordinaire, at your service."

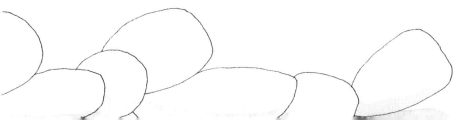

Swallowing hard, Victoria held up what was left of her kite. "Thanks for the offer, but my kite is ruined, and there's not enough time to make another."

The magician stroked his beard. "I have a solution if you don't mind a little help."

Victoria felt a ray of hope. "Do you really think we could make another kite? I'd give anything for a chance to beat Arnold Kropper for once, but the contest starts in ten minutes…"

The magician chuckled. "You just run along to that apple tree near the grandstand, and don't worry. This kite will beat them all—if it wants to."

"What do you mean?" Victoria started to ask, but Mr. Orsini had disappeared into the crowd.

As Victoria waited, Arnold walked by showing off his kite. "Hey, Measley Beasley, what happened to *your* kite?"

She gave him her meanest look. "As if you didn't know."

Laughing, Arnold walked on.

A moment later The Great Orsini appeared carrying a small case. When he opened it, Victoria was disappointed—no paper, no string, no sticks, only a jumble of bottles and boxes.

"But, Mr...."

"Quiet," said the magician, "I need to concentrate. Beeswax and butterscotch. Where is that recipe? Ah! Here we are. Two tablespoons of goose down, one pinch of eagle shell, a dash of eau de cumulus..." he mumbled as he poured and mixed.

"Please hurry, Mr. Orsini," urged Victoria. "They're getting ready to start, but we still don't have a kite."

The Great Orsini flung out his arms. "We will in exactly sixteen seconds."

A shimmering cloud swirled and sparkled in the air around Victoria. As it settled over her, her arms rose up and stood out straight. Her whole body grew stiff and narrow. Victoria had the strange feeling that she was disappearing. She watched with surprise as brilliant red paper appeared all around her.

The magician pulled a ball of string from his hat, tucked Victoria under his arm, and hurried past Arnold, who eyed them suspiciously as the announcer explained the rules.

"Each contestant may have three tries to get his or her kite into the air. The kites must remain airborne while the judges determine which is the highest and most daring. Good luck, and may the best kite win."

"Hey, Mr. Orsini," whispered Victoria, "you're crazy. I don't know the first thing about being a kite."

"Sure you do. You'll just be at the other end of the string. You'll love it. Now here we go—one, two, upsidaisy!"

Victoria felt the wind start to lift her, but a moment later she crashed back to earth. The magician brushed her off. "Tadpoles and tiddlywinks! I forgot a tail. Ah well, no harm done."

"Easy for you to say," mumbled Victoria.

Orsini pulled a string of scarfs from his sleeve. "There, that should do it."

Victoria closed her eyes tightly as she was again tossed upward. She rose steadily, but when she opened her eyes and saw Arnold's kite diving toward her, she gave a twist and headed for the ground.

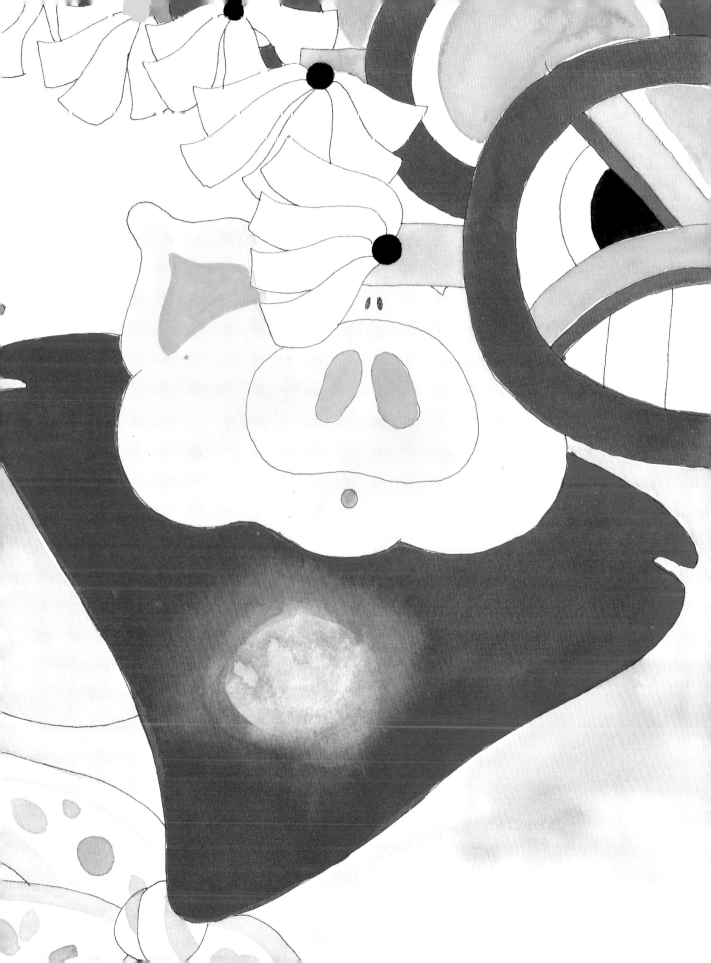

"What happened? You were doing beautifully."

"Oh, please, Mr. Orsini, it's just too scary. Can't you conjure up a real kite?"

"Do you want to win this contest or not? This is the only kite trick I know, and it just lasts for a little while, so let's get going. Think light! Think high! Think Arnold Kropper!"

Victoria took a deep breath. "Okay, Mr. Orsini, I'll give it one more try."

Once again Orsini threw Victoria into the air. With her eyes on the clouds, Victoria gained confidence as she rose. When she finally looked down, she gasped in wonder. Meadowbrook County spread below her like a patchwork quilt: golden squares of ripening fields, neat orchards, dense green areas of woods, the fair, the village, and beyond.

Her fears, the contest, even Arnold Kropper were forgotten as she experimented with twisting this way and that to catch the air currents. Her success left her giddy with delight. She'd never felt so light, so free.

Victoria flung herself into a series of daring swoops, glides, and loops that brought cheers from the spectators. She flew into a particularly strong breeze to climb even higher, when she suddenly was jerked to a halt instead. She strained desperately to escape, but the draft was too strong. Victoria felt her string pull tighter and tighter, then—snap! She shot up, did a triple somersault, and plunged toward the ground.

Using all of her newfound flying skills, Victoria managed to avoid crashing by twisting and turning with each passing breeze. Up then down, side to side, she fluttered through the fair. By the time she reached the end of the midway, she was feeling heavier, and it was more difficult to steer.

"Oh, no—I'm changing back to me."

With one last desperate glide, Victoria plunged into the apple tree and disappeared. Moments later a pale but smiling little pig climbed down.

"Are you Victoria Beasley?" one of the judges asked.
"Yes, Sir."
"Mr. Orsini was declared the winner just before his string broke, but he said to give the ribbon and this note to you."
Victoria looked around. Her new friend seemed to have disappeared. She opened the note.

Dear Victoria,
Sometimes winning takes a little magic and a lot of courage. Congratulations!

Your friend,
T.G. Orsini

Thanks for the shirttail, Robin!   BA

To Marvin, Cartoonist Extraordinaire.   RMK

Library of Congress Cataloging-in-Publication Data
Ayres, Becky.
Victoria flies high / Becky Ayres; illustrated by Robin Michal Koontz.
p.   cm.
Summary: With the help of a little magic, Victoria the pig is turned
into a kite which has a chance of winning the big kite-flying contest.
ISBN 0-525-65014-8
[1. Kites—Fiction.   2. Magic—Fiction.   3. Contests—Fiction.
4. Pigs—Fiction.]   I. Koontz, Robin Michal, ill.   II. Title.
PZ7. A9855Vi   1990
[E]—dc19   89-694
                                         CIP
                                         AC

Published in the United States by E.P. Dutton, New York, N.Y.,
a division of Penguin Books USA Inc.
Published simultaneously in Canada by Fitzhenry and Whiteside Limited, Toronto
Typography by Kathleen Westray
Printed in Hong Kong
First edition   10 9 8 7 6 5 4 3 2 1